Animal SOUP

With love and *buon appetito* to Milo and Phoebe Benwell-Froggatt – I.W.

For Tom, who likes soup – T.M.

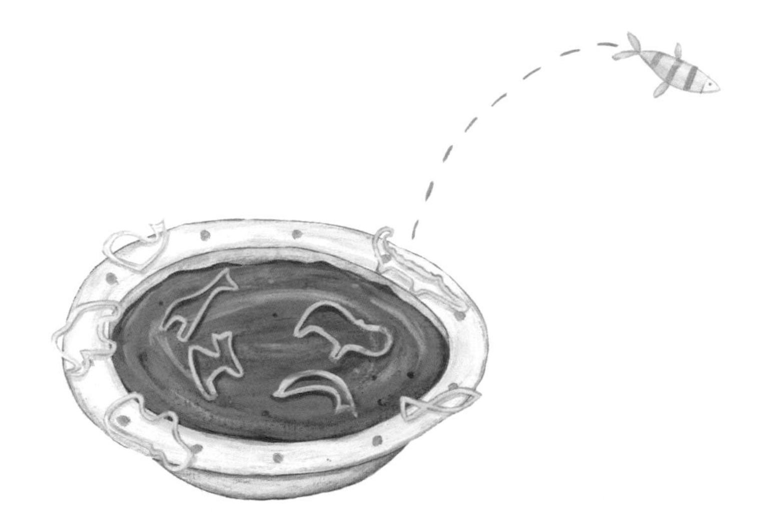

First published in the UK in 2007 by
Alison Green Books
An imprint of Scholastic Children's Books
Euston House, 24 Eversholt Street London NW1 1DB, UK
A division of Scholastic Ltd
London – New York – Toronto – Sydney – Auckland
Mexico City – New Delhi – Hong Kong

HB 10-digit ISBN: 0 439 94304 3
HB 13-digit ISBN: 978 0 439943 04 8
PB 10-digit ISBN: 0 439 94305 1
PB 13-digit ISBN: 978 0 439943 05 5

3 5 7 9 8 6 4

Printed in Singapore

Ian Whybrow Teresa Murfin

Animal Soup

ALISON GREEN BOOKS

Oliver's got some Animal Soup
With lots of animal shapes -
Of whales and hippos, crocodiles
And elephants and apes.

The trouble with giving him Animal Soup
Is that Oliver likes to play.

"Stop that, Oliver!"
cries his mum,
"Or I'll take that food away!"

But Oliver **loves** his Animal Soup
And rather than see it go,
He waves his wand,

jumps into a boat,

And he begins to row.

Now here is his soup and there is his chair,
So wherever can Oliver be?
There he goes! See him? Sailing away -
Like a sailor on the sea!

Mum says,
"Abracadabra!"
And makes herself
very small.

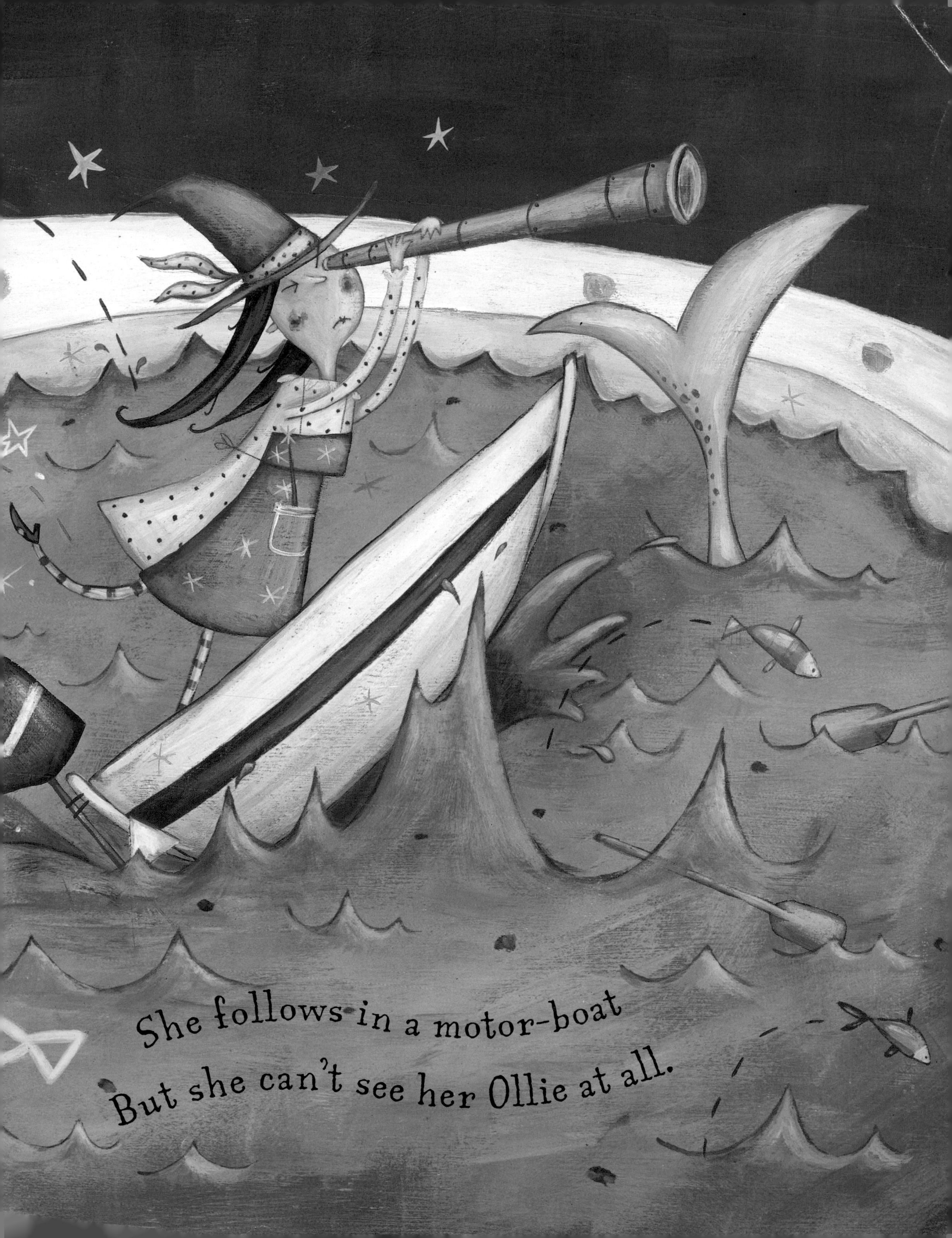

She follows in a motor-boat
But she can't see her Ollie at all.

Along comes a whale, a great big whale,
Swimming along on the tide.

"Open your mouth, Whale, let's have a look!
What have you got inside?"

"Good gracious,
it's an elephant!
But where's my darling son?

"Elephant!

Spit my Oliver out!

He's not a currant bun!"

Help!

A hippopotamus -

Terribly big and wide!

"Come along, Hippo, open your mouth.
Have **you** got my son inside?"

"Crikey!
It's a crocodile!
Look at his rows of teeth!"

Mum isn't scared.
She lifts up his jaw
To see what's underneath.

Can you believe it?

It's an ape!

"Is Oliver in your tummy?

"Open your mouth, Ape,
let's have a look!
And hurry!"
cries Oliver's mummy.

"I've got you, Oliver!" she calls.
"Thank goodness you're still whole!

“Is anything nasty
still lurking about?
Quick! - what have you got
in your bowl?”

Animal Soup!

Just Animal Soup –

The kind you get out of a tin!

And nothing disturbs young Oliver

Whenever he's tucking in.

Now the croc
and the hippopotamus
And the elephant,
ape and whale . . .

All come home for some Animal Soup . . .
And that's nearly the end of our tale.
Animal SOUP
Animal SOUP

But wasn't it silly of Oliver's mum
To leave those crackers out?
Animal SOUP
Animal SOUP
Animal SOUP
ANIMAL CRACKERS

Surely she knows
that a boy with a wand

Will want to
wave it about!